T. S. Moore

The vinedresser and other poems

T. S. Moore

The vinedresser and other poems

ISBN/EAN: 9783744722681

Printed in Europe, USA, Canada, Australia, Japan

Cover: Foto ©Andreas Hilbeck / pixelio.de

More available books at **www.hansebooks.com**

TO
MY PARENTS

CONTENTS

SENT FROM EGYPT WITH A FAIR ROBE OF TIS-SUE TO A SICILIAN VINEDRESSER.   B.C. 276
TO C. H. S.

PUT out to sea, if wine thou wouldest make
Such as is made in Cos : when open boat
May safely launch, advice of pilots take ;
And find the deepest bottom, most remote
From all encroachment of the crumbling shore,
Where no fresh stream tempers the rich salt wave,
Forcing rash sweetness on sage ocean's brine ;
As youthful shepherds pour
Their first love forth to Battos gnarled and grave,
Fooling shrewd age to bless some fond design.

Not after storm ! but when, for a long spell,
No white-maned horse has raced across the blue,
Put from the beach ! lest troubled be the well—
Less pure thy draught than from such depth were due.
Fast close thy largest jars, prepared, and clean !
Next weight each buoyant womb down through the flood,
Far down ! when, with a cord the lid remove,
And it will fill unseen,
Swift as a heart Love smites sucks back the blood :—
This bubbles, deeper born than sighs, shall prove.

If thy bowed shoulders ache, as thou dost haul—
Those groan who climb with rich ore from the mine ;
Labour untold round Ilion girt a wall ;
A god toiled that Achilles' arms might shine ;
Think of these things and double knit thy will !
Then, should the sun be hot on thy return,
Cover thy jars with piles of bladder weed,
Dripping, and fragrant still
From sea-wolds where it grows like bracken-fern :
A grapnel dragged will soon supply thy need.

Home to a tun convey thy precious freight !
Wherein, for thirty days, it should abide,
Closed, yet not quite closed from the air, and wait
While, through dim stillness, slowly doth subside
Thick sediment.   The humour of a day,
Which has defeated youth and health and joy,

3

Down, through a dreamless sleep, will settle thus,
Till riseth maiden gay,
Set free from all glooms past—or else a boy
Once more a school-friend worthy Troilus.

Yet to such cool wood tank some dream might dip :
Vision of Aphrodite sunk to sleep,
Or of some sailor let down from a ship,
Young, dead, and lovely, while across the deep,
Through the calm night, his hoarse-voiced comrades chaunt—
So far at sea, they cannot reach the land
To lay him perfect in the warm brown earth.
Pray that such dreams there haunt !
While, through damp darkness, where thy tun doth stand,
Cold salamanders sidle round its girth.

Gently draw off the clear and tomb it yet,
For other twenty days, in cedarn casks !
Where through trance, surely, prophecy will set ;
As, dedicated to light temple-tasks,
The young priest dreams the unknown mystery.
Through Ariadne, knelt disconsolate
In the sea's marge, so welled back warmth which throbbed
With nuptial promise : she
Turned ; and, half-choked through dewy glens, some great,
Some magic drone of revel coming sobbed.

Of glorious fruit, indeed, must be thy choice !
Such as has fully ripened on the branch,
Such as due rain, then sunshine, made rejoice,
Which, pulped and coloured, now deep bloom doth blanch !
Clusters like odes for victors in the games,
Strophe on strophe globed, pure nectar all !
Spread such to dry ! if Helios grant thee grace,
Exposed unto his flames
Two days, or, if not, three, or, should rain fall,
Stretch them on hurdles in the house four days !

Grapes are not sharded chestnuts, which the tree
Lets fall to burst them on the ground, where red
Rolls forth the fruit, from white-lined wards set free,
And all undamaged glows 'mid husks it shed ;

Nay, they are soft and should be singly stripped
From off the bunch, by maiden's dainty hand,
Then dropped through the cool silent depth to sink
(Coy, as herself hath slipped,
Bathing, from shelves in caves along the strand)
Till round each dark grape water barely wink ;

Since some nine measures of sea-water fill
A butt of fifty, ere the plump fruit peep,
Like sombre dolphin shoals when nights are still,
Which penned in Proteus' wizard circle sleep,
And 'twixt them glinting curves of silver glance
If Zephyr, dimpling dark calm, counts them o'er.
Let soak thy fruit for two days thus, then tread !
While bare-legged bumpkins dance,
Bright from thy bursting press arched spouts shall pour,
And gurgling torrents towards thy vats run red.

Meanwhile the maidens, each with wooden rake,
Drag back the skins and laugh at aprons splashed ;
Or youths rest, boasting how their brown arms ache,
So fast their shovels for so long have flashed,
Baffling their comrades' legs with mounting heaps.
Treble their labour ! still the happier they,
Who, at this genial task, wear out long hours,
Till vast night round them creeps,
When soon the torch-light dance whirls them away ;
For gods who love wine double all their powers.

Iacchus is the always grateful god !
His vineyards are more fair than gardens far ;
Hanging, like those of Babylon, they nod
O'er each Ionian cliff and hill-side scar !
While Cypris lends him saltness, depth, and peace ;
The brown earth yields him sap for richest green ;
And he has borrowed laughter from the sky ;
Wildness from winds ; and bees
Bring honey.—Then choose casks which thou hast seen
Are leakless, very wholesome, and quite dry !

That Coan wine the very finest is,
I do assure thee, who have travelled much

And learned to judge of diverse vintages.
Faint not before the toil ! this wine is such
As tempteth princes launch long pirate barks ;—
From which may Zeus protect Sicilian bays,
And, ere long, me safe home from Egypt bring,
Letting no black-sailed sharks
Scent this king's gifts, for whom I sweeten praise
With those same songs thou didst to Chloë sing !

I wrote them 'neath the vine-cloaked elm, for thee.
Recall those nights ! our couches were a load
Of scented lentisk ; upward, tree by tree,
Thy father's orchard sloped, and past us flowed
A stream sluiced for his vineyards ; when, above,
The apples fell, they on to us were rolled,
But kept us not awake.—O Laco, own
How thou didst rave of love !
Now art thou staid, thy son is three years old ;
But I, who made thee love-songs, live alone.

Muse thou at dawn o'er thy yet slumbering wife !—
Not chary of her best was nature there,
Who, though a third of her full gift of life
Was spent, still added beauties still more rare ;
What calm slow days, what holy sleep at night,
Evolved her for long twilight trystings fraught
With panic blushes and tip-toe surmise :
And then, what mystic might—
All, with a crowning boon, through travail brought !
Consider this and give thy best likewise !

Ungrateful be not !   Laco, ne'er be that !
Well worth thy while to make such wine 'twould be :
I see thy red face 'neath thy broad straw hat,
I see thy house, thy vineyards, Sicily !—
Thou dost demur, good, but too easy, friend :
Come put those doubts away ! thou hast strong lads,
Brave wenches ; on the steep beach lolls thy ship,
Where vine-clad slopes descend,
Sheltering our bay, that headlong rillet glads,
Like a stripped child fain in the sea to dip.

TO AN EARLY SPRING DAY

O DAY, thou found'st me sleeping ; let me sleep !
Too many of thy brothers too like thee
Have waked me with such manners.   Didst thou peep
With something of thy sisters' smile, may be,
I, even then, would sleep ; though they were gay
And called me oft in leafy flowery May :
Of banks more soft with moss than any bed,
With lush bee-peopled canopies o'er head,
They knew, and talking led me out to play.

Ah, they were gay, thy sisters !   They were young
And like the flowers, half divine with dew
Caught in their heads' loose roughened manes or flung
Forth in their frolic ; nothing sad they knew :
But thou, thou hast the sob of many sorrows,
Gloom from a stormy night thy wet wing borrows,
Each pelting shower, like angry sudden tears,
Answers an urgent spurring, which one hears,
Driving thee on toward disenchanted morrows.

Alas, there is but wind and rain abroad,
Fatiguing warmth that tempts the sharded buds !
I would I were a god of stone to hoard,
Like russet grange, the summer's golden floods,
All that Greece knew of beauty in her youth—
Handless and footless, from an isle aloof
Watching a main-land near across the sea,
Since heroes on white horses, buoyantly,
Chanting rode by to meet the dawn of truth.

Like some fair marble god, who pays no heed
To any day, in comely trance elate,
While honey-laden summers circling speed,
As echoes through a stone reverberate,
Thrilling his stillness—as a song is held
Spell-bound within the temple, where it swelled,
Long after all the choristers have ceased :
So would I be and never more released
To learn how men from such fair gods rebelled.

O Day, grey habited, thou too art sad !

Thou, too, art all too conscious of the past—
Of all those leaves that thy forerunners had
To bathe in, plunge in, fall to sleep at last,
Tired out like children, in !   Thou, with thy rain
Pelting wet roofs and dripping boughs, would'st fain
Dance among flowers and make the roses bob ;
Thou would'st from dells of thyme and clover rob
Scents to make sea-nymphs sniff and sniff again.

Then let us, Day, go friendly ! help thou me,
Strengthen my feet and occupy my hands,
And from all clinging yearning set me free,
To find in things the look that understands,
With mother-like alacrity, our need !
For nature is her children's friend indeed,
Who need not then be exiles anywhere,
But, loving beauty, still find beauty there,
As thou canst find thee comfort in thy speed.

Rough Minister of Life, thine infant hand
May once have ushered Psyche through Love's house.
Viewless and trembling didst thou later stand
And soothe her sleep with music? shy as mouse
Evade but when, with many a skyey leap
From cloud-caps downward, came, with meteor sweet,
Her rosy husband ?—Ah, attend my prayers,
Immediate as her unseen ministers,
Till hope grow real enough to clasp in sleep !

In sleep we can believe we, rapt and fain,
Full knowledge of illusive beauty store :—
In sleep, we do not know ourselves nor strain,
Like birds at sea and fainting ere the shore,
To reach a joy that, ever seeming near,
Lies far beyond our strength :—in sleep we hear,
As echoes hear, who do not weep at songs,
And unmoved watch, like stars, unpitied wrongs.
Then, Day, storm on till sleep be doubly dear !

Press on and shoulder up thy lagging clouds !
Invigour me !   Born from thine energy
And bright from thy despair, with leaves in crowds,

The spring shall be ! at last the spring shall be !
Beauty shall like a day-dream brave the light—
A day-dream likelier than the dreams of night,
Surmised among thy sisters, Summer Days,
When, 'mid birds singing, I will sing her praise
Exalting her with this thy strenuous might.

ROWERS' CHANT

ROW till the land dip 'neath
The sea from view.
Row till a land peep up,
A home for you.

Row till the mast sing songs
Welcome and sweet.
Row till the waves, out-stripped,
Give up dead beat.

Row till the sea-nymphs rise
To ask you why
Rowing you tarry not
To hear them sigh.

Row till the stars grow bright
Like certain eyes.
Row till the noon be high
As hopes you prize.

Row till you harbour in
All longing's port.
Row till you find all things
For which you sought.

SUMMER LIGHTNING

I WOULD rather ruffle leaves,
Pillaging a vine,
Than 'neath my tresses shelter thieves,
Robber lips at mine.

I would rather feel the rain,
When standing under cover,
Course my out-stretched hands a-main,
Than tears shed by a lover.

O Bird in the night awake,
Thou almost mak'st me weep.
Why should thy voice so shake?
Is it thy pinions ache?
What hindereth thee to sleep?
I want not to love and I will not . . . Oh!
Love's not worth so much! and thou dost know,
I know, and all the world too knows,
No girl need love unless she chose!

SILENCE SINGS

SO faint, no ear is sure it hears,
So faint and far ;
So vast that very near appears
My voice, both here and in each star
Unmeasured leagues do bridge between ;
Like that which on a face is seen
Where secrets are ;

Sweeping, like veils of lofty balm,
Tresses unbound
O'er desert sand, o'er ocean calm,
I am wherever is not sound ;
And, goddess of the truthful face,
My beauty doth instil its grace
That joy abound.

THE YOUNG CORN IN CHORUS

ALL we, the young corn, stalwart stand
In millions upright side by side,
And countless acres of the land
In orderly close chorus hide,
Shouting : " Gold, of his largess,
And health he discharges
Both far and wide."

Though all the world were brimmed with gold
And valleys with health had over-run,
Who could command his hand to hold,
Contest the giving of the Sun ?
Hail him ; vigour for growing
He cometh bestowing
On each weak one !

The Winds with showers on their backs,
His servants, lounge by distant seas,
And far-seen summits of their packs
Heave up when shifted for their ease ;
Wearied ; long there attending
Lest heat of his sending
Cloy those he would please.

LOVE-LIES-BLEEDING

LOVE lies bleeding ;
Fever is feeding
On flesh which swords have stricken.
Should sweet blood clot and thicken ?
How could they slay him so,
When were pleading
Such eyes as his, you know?
Such eyes, such woe !

DOUBTFUL DAWN

WAKE, Love; I am early woken!
Ah, Love, I am ignorant whether,
So many hearts as thou hast broken,
In aught thou canst be clever:
Will he for ever
Love me, this man thou has set in my heart?
Will he be true? shall I bear a true part?

Wake, Love; I am ready: waken!
Love, follow thou me till time's ending!
So many hearts as thou hast forsaken,
Thou must needs be in want of befriending—
Have foes a-bending
Brows on thee:—come, come into my heart;
Take shelter; turn good and oh! never depart!

WOODSTOCK MAZE

A CROWN in her lap ; all proud of her bower ;
A woman become a child from using power
Her beauty gave her, bounteous gave ; and thence
Renewed in petulance and lucky faults ;
So fresh, her whole life breathless halts
To see a star fall through immense
High arch'd twilight—
Rosamund peaceful sat and sang,
While the woods lay still and their echoes rang
To the song " Love loves the night."

A captive to innocence, held there, to wait
Pale, where the paths all led, whence none led straight
Or could help flight, until the queen came up
And told her in a whisper she must die,
Hated, beneath the quiet sky.
Slowly she drained the deep-stained cup,
And still grew white
Slowly, there, where she sat and sang,
While still the wooded echoes rang
To the song " Love loves the night."

SEMELE

SEMELE lay in bliss all night,
Loved and loving without light,
Blind but tingling like a string
Struck by dying poet when
Glorified he ceases sing
Listened to by gods and men.

Semele dared a wish,—to see ;
That her eyes might equals be
With her heart and lips and ears :
Night on perfect night she pled.
Sudden lightning drank her tears,
Life and sweetness : she lay dead.

Semele dying thus yet bare
Fiery rapid Bacchus fair
Who, nursed by goddesses and in
High heaven reared, hath since progressed
Throughout all Asia with the din
Of cymbal, drum and voice possessed.

10

" BEAUTIFUL nymph all white with fear,
Live with me, love with me, lie with me here,
A night, a month, a year ! "
" Shepherd, shepherd, I am loved ; I am cursed !
And the ills I have suffered are far from the worst."

" Corals have I who dwell in a cave ;
White trembler, though brown as a rock, I am brave;
Break over my breast, sad wave ! "
" Fisher, fisher, I am chased ; I am blessed !
Yet the joys I have tasted are far from the best."

" Her youth peeped through her tattered cloak !
She was white ; we are black, we Ethiop folk ;
She shuddered when we spoke ! "
" Great Zeus, great Zeus ! I am thine, I am pure !
Thy touch but not theirs, will my soul endure ! "

" White Cloud, no more driven !   O Feminine Youth,
Rest ! oaks at Dodona have told thee the truth,
Thou shalt bear me a son in sooth ! "
" Grandly, grandly I am loved ; I am kissed ;
At my beauty, the eyes of the stars all mist ;
Argus is dead ;
A warm wind sighs ;
Egypt, our noble bed,
Hushed, nuptial and secret lies ;
I am sure, I can feel, that my cheeks are red—
Are kissed and red ! "

A DUET

"FLOWERS nodding gaily, scent in air,
Flowers posied, flowers for the hair,
Sleepy flowers, flowers bold to stare—"
"Oh, pick me some."

"Shells with lip, or tooth, or bleeding gum,
Tell-tale shells, and shells that whisper 'Come,'
Shells that stammer, blush, and yet are dumb—"
"Oh, let me hear."

"Eyes so black they draw one trembling near,
Brown eyes, caverns flooded with a tear,
Cloudless eyes, blue eyes so windy clear—"
"Oh, look at me."

"Kisses sadly blown across the sea,
Darkling kisses, kisses fair and free,
Bob-a-cherry kisses 'neath a tree—"
"Oh, give me one."

Thus sang a king and queen in Babylon.

TO SLOW MUSIC
LIKE shovels white of porcelain
In pyramids of spices deep,
Are shells half scooped into brown sand
Which ebbing waves drew on a heap.
Like blush by smooth nail overlain
Are others ; five for either hand,
Nay plenty for both hands and feet
Of Venus when she walks the strand
Escaped from perfumed Temple's heat.

Like wail which for Adonis rang,
Drawn up and round a hollow maze,
In others dwells a wealth of sound
That she prefers to all men's praise.
Made coral by a moment's pang
And snapt off from true hearts are found
The branching red rich veins of those
Who, wounded by her son, have drowned,
Seeking a "sea-change" for their woes.

The idle nymphs in caves far down,
Secluded life-long from alarms,
Where distance lulls the billow's roar
And moony sea-light dreams of day,
Made every shell that strews the shore.
They with their handywork do crown
Long tresses—twine their grand white arms
With chains of cowries, and array
Their necks and bosoms. . . . Naught of lily
(Since Venus never tells) know they,
Naught of the tender violet's charms,
Of daisy naught, nor daffodilly.

A WINNOWER OF CORN TO THE WINDS
FROM THE FRENCH OF JOACHIM DU BELLAY

I OFFER ye, troop light and gay,
Who passing wing your way,
As round the world you make,
And, with a murmur soothing
Through shady verdure moving,
Set all to gently shake—

I offer ye these violets,
Lilies and lesser pets,
These roses here pell-mell—
These red and splendid roses
Buds which to-day uncloses—
These opening pinks as well.

With your soft breathing far and wide
Freshen our country side,
Freshen my dwelling too ;
The while toil is unmanning
My strength, o'er corn bent fanning
The hot and long day through.

THE PANTHER
TO C. S. R.

CONSIDER now the panther : Such the beast
On which the naked feet of Circe rest—
Her footstool wherein anger is increased
For ever, yet for ever is suppressed.

Sleek, powerful, and treacherous, and cowed,
With amber eyes like tears that watch a lamp—
A Queen's tears, thwarted by remembrance proud,
Clear cut as gold-coins that her mint doth stamp.

How politic is grace in moods morose !
This smooth composure waits but our caress ;
'Tis pride put on to beggar love ; there glows
Knit with this strength some utter tenderness.

That blunt round paw, and padded glove-like palm !
How strange, if, there, like dulled assassin steel,
Sheathed claws wait ready ! Thus in forest calm
That cruel face the ferns' arched fronds conceal.

Then all is glowing, like deep-treasured glee :
E'en butterflies might settle on this coat ;
The shy gazelles may snuff full gingerly,
Rich blossoms drown the odours they should note.

The holy Baobab, with grey blue stems
And aisled vistas solemn as a church,
Denies this presence, and this life condemns ;
Its meek-eyed throngs would wrong it should they search.

A bound ! a scamper ! cry ! the sob of death !
And these claws open up the heart, that pang
Had filled to bursting with a last gasped breath ;
Warm blood is lapped, and fleshed is every fang :

Hereto conspired the beauty of the place,
Whose whole consent seemed given to life's ease.
Thus, by a garden walk, some poppy's grace
Brings down a child Sultana to her knees ;

Whose tall indifference next prompts her fond hand
To stoop its cup, where drowsy drops of dew

Roll and unite like quick-silver, or stand
In lustrous clots, then self-divide anew :

All, with a kiss, her human heart soon must
Attempt to possess ; or quaff, with amorous sip,
Those wilful gems freighted with purple dust,
Where lurks a bee-sting venomed for her lip ;

For while large petals closed at shut of eve,
The bee ceased not to gorge—could not burst free—
Fumed through the night, and stingless took his leave.
Thus rage in this beast pent left perfidy.

II

BUT, lo ! they yawn, those wide-hinged python jaws,
Unroof the rose-pink ivory-studded bed,
Where, like a languid flame, the lithe tongue draws
Its moist caress round gums and hollows red.

Dost, cloyed by rich meats spicy as the south,
Expose thy fevered palate to the cool,
Which, like snow melting in an emperor's mouth,
Helps make excess thy life's ironic rule ?

Soft-coated, each curved ear seems some weird flower,
Whose gulf with silken lashes gleams replete ;
Such yield to let the fond fly, feasting, lower,
But close and stiffen to forbid retreat.

Thus dost thou draw our thought, by subtler hints,
Still further down the vortex of thy spell ;
Lace-winged on delicate feet it onward glints—
A trickling tear—a soul hung over hell.

Those cushion brows, with sullen show of thought,
Deceive the eye ; so emery, cloaked in state
Of some mock scarlet berry needle-wrought,
Maketh a young child marvel at its weight.

Can they be vacant? Can thy strong neck raise,
Without the aid of magic, thy full brain?
Of thee our child-thought in the mind delays,
Whence to dislodge it reason toils in vain.

The mystery of evil and its charm
Prevail, like beauty, radiant from thy form ;
Thou art an enemy that can disarm
Man's arrogance, which like a swollen storm

Sweeps all creation with the tyrant force
Of his long hunger for congenial dreams ;
Though he condemn thee, yet as in remorse
He thy soft pelt a couch for beauty deems—

Spreadeth it for the bride, his ecstasy
Crowns "Rose of Sharon, Lily of the valleys"—
Voweth it doth become her, likening thee,
Soul of the woods, to her, soul of his palace.

TEMPIO DI VENERE
A MARBLE ruin nigh forgotten
Fronts sheer on Naples' bay ;
Its cornice stones are weather-rotten,
Stained both by rain and spray.

Its steps the mounting shore has buried,
All save the top-most three,
To which small waves run up like hurried
Sly kisses of the sea.

Its fluted columns crevice-jointed
Must totter every storm.
Bird-droppings have its eaves anointed,
Blunted each moulding's form.

A wreckage mast, its only rafter,
Supports an old tanned sail.
Here Venus dwelt who so loved laughter ;
Here now chinks flute and wail.

Here once the pirate-Pompey's seaman
Offered her shells and gold ;
Here oft-flogged slave or pious leman
Complained that hearts are sold.

With pavement chequer-rich sand-whitened,
Which tell-tales flaws of wind—
With walls, that once gay pictures brightened,
Blank as an old man's mind—

For fisher's painted boat 'tis stable,
Festooned with nets and cords,
Littered with dead-eyes, ends of cable,
Crab-baskets, boat-hooks, boards.

No more here marble limbs shall glisten,
Nor carved face smile here more,
And, bending forward half to listen,
Prompt those who mute adore.

Yet, though he call no goddess mother,
A child bathed here to-day
Who, naked, was as Cupid's brother,
So sturdy arch and gay !

DAPHNE

NOT avaricious was that chastity,
That saved its treasure at such sovran cost
Of promise snapt right through and beauty lost :
She fled in lavish love of what might be.

Such love is the prime instinct Nature owns ;
It yearns upon perfection through each form,
Compels winged birds to keep their hard eggs warm,
In boy's heart-worship grown-man's strength enthrones.

She had experienced growth, she had been born,
Not goddess-like dawned perfect ; and her feet
With every forward movement helped complete
Her realm ; her reign waxed stable morn by morn.

No need she knew, save freedom to unfold
And foster her rich native dower ; she knelt
At no shrine anxious to be heard, and felt
No fear save Hope's, whose fears refine to gold.

Her worship flowed in song ; by day and night
She duly profited ; her open face
And gracious carriage no uneasy trace
Of haste betrayed; and sound health proved her right.

She, flawlessly advanced, ne'er sought release
From the strict round of culturing exercise ;
Her hour was not yet come ; avoiding eyes
Scarce apt to understand, she haunted trees.

Encountered with his uncontrolled desire,
Her whole Hope thus thrown roughly on suspense—
As yearning mother's hopes are fears intense—
Lent her the panic white and speed of fire.

Such timely aid for suicidal power
She could not know ; the transformation came :—
A living ash left by pure passion's flame,
The nymph once vanished, see the laurel tower !

II

LESS than the best, can that suffice a god ?
She was too true to dream it ; ne'er before

Had failed, nor knew how soon remorse will nod—
Sleep show the soul, nor gall its hardened sore,
Peeps of lost paradise as through a swinging door.

The water that had bathed her, the white dress
That floated round her noble attitudes,
Were sister-natures and their right express :
But Love, that stoops to violence, obtrudes
The lie on Beauty's health, dismays her marble moods.

Had she dared give the pittance he desired
(Nay, tried to snatch !), her past must straight have frowned :
Although the god of that he gained ne'er tired,
Although by prosperous years she had been crowned,
While Memory walked behind, she ne'er had dared look round.

Ah ! have concessions proved of so much worth?
A life is saved, a martyr has been lost ;
An earthy mother, teeming like the earth,
Gained, but a white nymph's story is the cost ;
Millions admit so soon, that their best hopes are crossed.

The multitudes of failure march with sound,
To Love's divine desire and Youth's great zeal
Callous ; they have been young and loved, they found
It folly all.   Why should to Beauty kneel
The very plain? to Truth those who must needs conceal?

SEPTEMBER TWILIGHT

A LARGE pool, and tall trees, and lo ! undressed
One runs out, pauses, hesitates, looks round :
Twilight reviveth freedom long oppressed ;
The bather plunges in ; a generous sound
And radiant splash of waters welcome him ;
His wake all silver widens, he can swim !

—Swim in that dark cold water—swim and wend
As through a dream with strange facility,
A dream still quite unconscious it must end,
Quite dreadless—though this pool proved open sea,
No memory goes with it, no hope leads,
But inwardly content it onward speeds.

FROM THE FRENCH OF ARTHUR RIMBAUD

ON summer evenings blue, where ears of wheat
Peck at you, I shall pass and spare grass tread—
Dreaming, shall feel its freshness round my feet,
And let the wind keep bathing my bare head.

I shall not speak, naught shall I think about,
But infinite love will flood my whole soul through ;
Far I shall wander, gipsy-like far out
In Nature ; happy as with a woman too.

LES CHERCHEUSES DE POUX

WHEN, forehead full of torments hot and red,
The child invokes white crowds of hazy dreams,
Two sisters tall and sweet draw near his bed,
Whose fingers frail nails tip with silv'ry gleams.

The child before a window open wide,
Where blue air bathes a maze of flowers, they sit ;
And in his heavy hair dew falls, while glide
Their fingers terrible with charm through it.

So hears he sing their breath a dread hush curbs ;
How rich with rose and leafy sweets it is !
It sometimes a salival lisp disturbs
On the lip drawn back, or deep desires to kiss.

Through perfumed silences their lashes black
Beat slow ; from soft electric fingers he,
In colourless grey indolence, hears crack
'Neath tyrant nails the death of each small flea.

Then wells in him the wine of idleness,
Delirious power, th' harmonica's soft sigh :
The child still feels to their long drawn caress
Ceaselessly heave and swoon a wish'to cry.

JUDITH

WHAT have you in your apron wrapped?
Your face is fell with fright;
Your shadow hurries to catch you up,
Across the blank moonlight.

Why is your maid so white and wan?
What makes her so alert?
Why with her hands does she fumble thus
And wipe them on her skirt?

Ill to be borne your burden seems,
You fetch your breath so short;
Why do your eyes shine brighter far
Than, for the moon, they ought?

You take less heed of what you pass
Than one who walks in a dream;
The thing you hide so fills you out,
A woman with child you seem.

You take a turn, the town you see,
Your feet to run begin;
Is yours the strength which makes so strong
The supple thews of sin?

Why beat you now with naked hands?
On the gate they make no sound;
Your knuckles bleed; ah! your force fails;
You drop upon the ground.

Now you are raised upon your feet
And pulled within the town;
Wild light from flickering flames falls full
Upon your bloody gown;

Your throat is thrilled, your tongue is thick,
And triumph turns your lip;
As men tumultuous throng you round,
Each girds a sword to his hip:

But now by your imperious cries
Were they roused up from bed;
Now, high above your head, your hands
Hold Holofernes' head.

THE SIBYL

MY heart no more within me dwells,
'Tis grown too big for me ;
Now every vein my body holds
Feeds from immensity ;
The pain I feel does pulse, be sure,
Through boundless air and sea.

And, should I die, a rain of blood
Would be the fearful sign
That all my words of knowledge are
And not offspring of wine ;
For my heart fills the whole blue world,
The sunset's blood is mine.

And, if my hate of you should grow
And fill my brain with heat,
And blind mine eyes and throttle me,
Beware for your fields of wheat !
My rage can guide the black hailstorm
And the trampling of his feet.

If, as you stole my love from me,
My love with wilful eyes,
The boy, him who would listen long
And nod his head as wise
When I read from the scriptured scroll
Those ancient words I prize—

(I knew he hardly understood—
That he but loved my voice :
I loved his playful speaking hands,
His happy helpful choice
Of word or tone to meet my mind ;
His kiss made me rejoice)

If, as you stole him, then, I say,
And took him to your wars
And let the sword of an enemy
Work this hell-deed of yours—
If I should long for another kiss,
Lust's kiss to heal Love's sores :—

Then flame-like would my frenzy be,
As a three months' summer-drought,
When all green things turn brown or grey
For all the springs give out,
While your young men like parched up grass
Would faint in its fever's rout.

The sun, I say, is one with me ;
And clouds are but my limbs ;
And as my veins all water-ways,
For through them my will swims ;
So any day the floods may come—
Go chant your prayerful hymns !

NIOBE

" BEHOLD me what I am, behold !
And Leto—look on her !
More beautiful, and crowned with gold
More copious than her hair."

" Mother, though the sky keep blue,
The fields take on an ashen hue,
For terribly sudden and cold it blew,
The gust that seemed to answer you !"

" Behold my seven sons, behold
My daughters seven and fair !
More lovely these, and those more bold
Than Leto's far-famed pair."

" Mother, though sunshine cover you,
Your lips have trembled and changed hue,
Till, letting those ringing accents through,
They shook and we were shaken too !"

" Behold my husband's bed, behold
Her god-dishonoured lair !
My births draw honest eyes like gold
From off her ill-got pair."

" Mother, I am stricken through !"
" And I, pain drags mine eyelids to !"
" They slay us, who our brothers slew
And god-like curled the lip at you !"

" Behold me what I am, behold !
And Leto—look on her !
My utter woe told and retold
Shall curse her cruel pair !"

CHORIC FRAGMENTS
I. THE DYING SWAN

OH silver-throated Swan
Struck, struck ! a golden dart
Clean through thy breast has gone
Home to thy heart.
Thrill, thrill ! O silver throat,
O silver trumpet, pour
Love for defiance back
On him who smote ;
And brim—brim o'er
With love ; and ruby-dye thy track
Down thy last living reach
Of river, sail the golden light·—
Enter the sun's heart—even teach,
O wondrous-gifted Pain, teach thou
The god to love, let him learn how.

II. THE HOME OF HELEN

LACEDAEMON, hast thou seen it?
Lacedaemon, Lacedaemon!
From Taÿgetus the forests
Slope from snows raised far above them!
Lacedaemon rich in corn-lands,
With the grand hill-shoulders round them
Blue as lapis in the twilight,
Striking early every morning
Through the mist till when the azure
Drops a veil of lucent sapphire
O'er our mountains in the noon-tide—
Our old ramparts, walls of safety!

And Eurotas—hast thou heard him,
Heard Eurotas, old Eurotas,
Gurgle, growl and gnaw the boulders?
Hast thou heard Eurotas laughing?
Hast thou stemmed his solemn current,
Where the dark rose-laurels shade it,
In the cool cliff-sheltered places,
Where the women bathe, while gravely
Swans sail in and out among them—
Swimming women, in pure water
Passing 'neath swans proud and passive,
Where Zeus saw and loved white Leda?

III. A CHORUS OF DORIDES

DEAD, dead, hale youth is dead,
Broken, bruised, broken, bathed in spray.
See, see, the hair, the wealth of his head,
With spoilt wreath-tendrils wed!
Limp as a dress once gay
Which on the shore is found
Where bathing a child has drowned,
So lies he white as the spray;—
So white Adonis lay
Before his whimpering hound;
So white on mid-sea lone
Rocked by the billows lay
Fallen Icarus—Phæthon fallen,
Through flaming forest, prone,
Deaf to the wail at dawn,
To houseless nymph and fawn—
Deaf where the leaves were ashes,
All lifeless, white; and so
Lay Hyacinth, his pillow
Tragic with purple splashes,
Deaf to left-handed Woe,
Where breezes through the willow
On beds of blue-bells blow.
Were these not kissed?—not washed with tears?
Did any fond name at their ears
Fail to plead vainly?

.　　.　　.　　.　　.　　.　　.

Dead, dead, poor short-lived lover,
Wasted, wrecked, wasted; day by day
Two careless tides will cover
And roll thee in their spray.
When piecemeal grow thy frail bones white,
Wilt thou through thy worn skull by night
Hear shore-wind sighing?

.　　.　　.　　.　　.　　.

CHORUS OF GRECIAN GIRLS

WE maidens are older than most sheep,
Though not so old as the rose-bush is ;
We are only as pretty as that.
We are gay as the weather.   Our minds are deep
Like wells, as any boy tells
By the blushes he dares not kiss.
The hills are fond of our chat.
We dance and shake like ringing bells,
Till our hair tumbles out of our hoods.
Our feet are bare, our feet are bare ;
But we don't care, we don't care,
For the boys are away in the woods,
Hunting the boar or bear.
We pretend to fly
Up into the sky,
Jumping with both feet together,
Holding out like wings
Our sleeves and things :
Feeling as light as a feather,
We don't wonder whether
The day is long
Or the night short,
Since all our thought,
Is but big as the song
Of a brown fussy bee,
And just fills the flower which we
Each call " Me."

CHORUS OF MAIDENS ON GILEAD

"THOU hast brought me very low ;
For I—I have no son
And other daughter none."
Moaned Jephthah in his woe.

So moaned he in his woe ;
But the host of the Lord helped ours
In the thunder-laden weather ;
And their daughters, our slaves, are as flowers
Lashed by the black hail showers ;
Of their dead they have help again never.
Their jewels round our necks are hung ;
We shall be brides and mothers :
No alien spoil she wore—though young,
She set no store by lovers ;
But wandered two months on the hills,
And bathed at dawn by lonely rills,
Wailing her virginity,
All her promise unfulfilled,
All her beauty's dignity,
All her skill, that nothing skilled,
Though she knew how to fashion clothes—
How to broider robes with silk—
How to knead and leaven loaves—
How to cream and curdle milk.

Though a mother, though a mother ne'er,
Yet praise we her.—
Though a maiden, though a maiden, thou
Hast glory now.—
Oh, the grass that springs from earth
By clear-shining after rain !
Oh, the light that comes to birth
In a cloudless dawn again !

Doomed she roamed with her companions fair,
Sleeping in the open air ;
Wand'ring through the April twilights warm,
Touching notes upon a shawm :—
Chanting, when the morning throbbed with light,

Robed and solemn all in white,
Came upon the shepherds lonely ;
For the awed and reverent eyes
Of lone men and lone men only,
Took knowledge of her exercise—
Watched, athwart the almond screen,
White feet dance on the young grass—
Watched heads crowned with lilies pass,
O'er a hedge of laurels green—
Heard the sad hill-echo call
A tale of maidens by their names—
Heard themselves one moment laugh,
And stopped short upon his path
Listening long : but that was all ;
Doomed at outset were their games.
Likewise, maidens, likewise, we stop short,
Checked by a thought ;
Sought as brides we, sought as brides, all cry—
" Ah thou must die !
To Jehovah thou wast vowed,
When thy father spake aloud,
Swearing he would sacrifice
Whate'er first should greet his eyes
On returning home, if he
Might be blessed with victory :
Sad he was and sad are we."·

Oh, the grass that springs from earth
By clear-shining after rain !
Oh, the light that comes to birth
On a cloudless morn again !
We wear their jewels in our ears ;
We shall be brides and mothers :
But first we shed for thee our tears ;
Unmindful of our lovers,
We wander four days on the hills
And bathe at dawn by lonely rills.

PHANTOM SEA-BIRDS

SIRS, though ocean's gapless bound
Ever-same do gird us round,
With the East-wind at our back,
Ere the tilting blue turn black,
Fix the eye on glowing haze
Which the sun's late-lingering rays
Crimson like anemones
That butterflies in woodland kiss.
Of unmoored island on these seas
I have heard there rumour is:
Though the prow duck to the dips,
And abrupt waves slap the ship's
Bellied bows whose timber thrills,
We may see its poppied hills,
Safe in ward of magic, steer,
Summer-sweet, o'er surges drear,
With the rambling palace, rich
Home of Circe, island-witch,
Daughter of the misled Sun,
Whom false Persa lured and won,
Long held fast and kissed and kissed,
Having couched her like a mist,
Where the salt, waste, marshy fens
Find sea-monsters brackish dens:
Helios lay there on the rushes
Which the booming storm-wind crushes,
Blushing gorgeously for shame—
Lay for hours all the same.—
Hark, perhaps a Siren sings,
Viewless talons, tail and wings;
Deadly, deadly now their charm
With no outward show of harm.
Listen, listen, back the ear
With the hollow hand, to hear.

" The air is alive, yet fear no ill;
Let the helm loose, and trust our skill;
Free the tugging sail with a jerk,
For we can do all manner of work.

Safe as a bubble on milk new drawn,
Drift like a curled moon before the dawn.
Dreams that merge in a dream more vast,
Your lives shall merge in life at last,
Where death shall loom no more but frame the past,
As frames a park an open palace-door,
Where leaves blown in ne'er reach across the floor
To kings whose minds hark back, but their wounds grow not
                                                        sore.

Fear, there, seems childish passion, known no longer ;
Each sense has leisure ; memory, though stronger,
Yet veils what else might tempt the fond heart to deplore.
A queen shall fill the crystal up with wine,
To bathe your lips still smarting from the brine ;
And you shall tread,
Bare-foot, on petals shed ;
And you shall lie in jasmine-trellised bed,
Dream, meet with any friend alive or dead ;
Obedient sleep,
Prolonged for rapture deep,   .
Shall let each soul her chosen comrade keep
And to the full in boon communion steep :
Turn once to hear,
True lips will brush your ear,
Our bodies in your arms be real and dear—
One whom you loved in vain at last drawn near.

" Woe ! woe !
Let honey flow,
Let the sharp blush come and go,
Draw thick drops from the breast's too passive snow.
O talons, let
A warm red rainfall wet
The unmoved faces, dew the stiff beard's jet !
Ere it be vain,
Choke down this sobbing pain !
Sing, with the lips where many found great gain,
The whole of love,
The births and deaths thereof,
Timed to the wings of some spray-drenchèd dove,

Whose pink feet dip
In the long wave's eager lip,
While faintness numb invades each frail plume-tip !—
Love, in our arms
We nurse and lull thy'qualms,
Yet never felt or feel thy sovereign charms.
Our hearts are cold ;
Love, a new tale, was told
In our young ears—now has the tale grown old,
Love still unknown,
Whose praise, and that alone,
Has mocked our ears : our hearts are still our own.
Those who praised him,
Knit with us limb in limb,
Died blind with bliss while yet our eyes were dim.
Still would we try,
Before our sweetness fly,
With you to capture Love, share Love, and die."

Turn, turn with a welling tear
And a pleasure-cozened ear :—
See the huge black canvas bars
Half the fully-wakened stars,
While the tackle's tarry smell
Faintly from the hold doth tell.
Ah ! the bleak mid-ocean plain,
Sad Persephone's cold field,
Heaves with no rich golden grain,
But salt tears and sleep its yield.—
Queen, now on these furrows rocked,
May our brains from dreams be locked.

ON A PICTURE BY PUVIS DE CHAVANNES

A SPACIOUS land lies large in broad daylight ;
Where warm wind healthily goes to and fro,
As here a woman dear might come and go ;
In courtesy the trees incline their height,
Rustling their robes as folk at a wedding might ;
And full of flowers the grass, by scythes laid low,
Scents the sunshine, while pores the fond willow
Over pride's paradise in waters bright.
A patriarchal people dwell in peace
And plenty, perfect without wealth's increase ;
Nursed in the lap of lowland hills, their homes
Are gay with flowers ; both morn and evening airs
Are guests within their doors ; and for their prayers
Cows safely calve, bees build big honey-combs.

SAPPHO'S DEATH
ON THREE PICTURES BY GUSTAVE MOREAU

I

AMID a wilderness of rock-piled towers
She sits; dank raiment shudders o'er her grace;
A damp from Lethe doth its pride efface:
Chilled through she sits and waits impending hours.
Her dark loosed hair is crowned with heavy flowers;
One cold hand grips her unhewn throne; in place
The other keeps her falling veil; her face
Is trodden battlefield of passion's powers.
—Sits quiet and complains of nobody:
No anguished sighs her tortured lips dispart;
But always in her ears and through her heart
The waves a ceaseless cruel parody
Of her last fruitless love-song chant and sing,
Nor will her sore heart deaden to their sting.

II

WITH hands vibrating, with lips trembling still,
Her sister heart and lute strings snapt in twain,
In one chord struck and overtaxed by pain,
She falls; and her dark gowns with salt wind fill,
Like those black sails which turned the sunshine chill
For Minotaur-doomed crews—fill too in vain:
Her bare feet fall and gleam like gulls new-slain
'Mid gulls who hoarsely shriek an omen ill:
She falls, as through a dream's suspense that strains
The moment's heart with time's immensity—
As down Truth's well fond cups whence Hope ne'er gains
The draught that quencheth thirst's entirety:
She falls, but her voice soars and yet remains—
Suspends her yet in immortality.

III

STILLED is the sea, the cliffs stand hugely still,
While the sun dies; but in the sky a crowd
Of tattered banners desolate, mute, and proud,
Marshalling, honours his departing skill.

Love strove with Song, and Love has now his will ;
Apollo's forces have drawn off, and loud,
Afar, Love hails his dame ; her foe has bowed ;
Save those sad clouds at Lesbos, all is still.
Yet pulses of white wings loom o'er the deep
Unanimous in steady-purposed quest
Of Sappho, who at last finds peace in sleep.
The first stoops o'er her now as o'er its nest :
From Paphos' dovecotes come they here to keep
A pious vigil at their queen's behest.

53
HOPE

HOPE is a dream dreamed by the mummied past,
Or sound inside an egg ; loved hearts with ours
To wed—as some bee-go-between the flowers—
She woman-like e'er walketh over-fast,
Half-frightened by odd shadows that are cast
In front from just behind ; hers are all powers
By which the unknown helps the known ; she towers
Where through the rainbow we would stride at last.
The solemn snow and silver hair are hers,
For folded linen clothes and napkins wrapped
Together by themselves : each neat bud bears
Witness to her deft fingers, who ne'er tapped
At Memory's door and found her smileless—kissed
Blind Love and left unfound the path he missed.

SONNET DE RONSARD POUR HÉLÈNE
LIVRE II., NO. XLII

WHEN you, quite old, by night with candles, well
Up to the fire, wind skeins or spin, you'll keep
Crooning my verse and, plunged in wonder deep,
Say " Ronsard fames days when I was a belle."
And you will have no servant hearing tell
Such news, though bowed with labour half-asleep,
But shall, at sound of Ronsard, waking leap,
Blessing your name by praise made durable.
I, under ground and with nor bone nor thew,
A shade shall rest near shadow myrtles ; you
Will by the hearth, old, crouching, scarce be blithe,
My love—your proud disdain for constant sorrows.
Live now, believe me, wait for no to-morrows ;
Pluck even to-day the roses of your life.

ALCESTIS

" O GLAD Devotion going up the sky,
Dawn brighter than a child's best mornings are,
Art seen, yet deemed for human strength too far?
We, prone to view an end, of Hope too shy—
Too diffident, await Fate's casting die
Much as Fear waits.   Westward speeds every star ;
Some, which set quick upon the sun, there are
Drop into it ; those glory, so may I.
Love should not barter like coarse traffickers
And count devotion gold to buy in store
Of helps—nay, oft my children thank me for
Some boon not mine to give nor really theirs :
Let me, a child, own gifts in everything,
Like them blow kisses to the birds that sing."

PYGMALION

TO work at sunrise nor till sunset rest,
Week's end spliced in week's end : 'twas thus he wrought ;
And I have often seen him in my thought
With eager bare arms leant across her breast
To chisel chin or cheek, while, where they pressed,
His labour's sweat made bright the marble bust.
Till lo ! she stands amid the work-shop dust
In proudest pose of loveliness undressed.
His work once stayed, he, weakened by long strife,
Falls like a swathe from summer-heat's keen scythe :
So sees he, waking at the day's decease,—
Not the sea-mothered Mother of all life,
Then vanished—but, alone, alive, he sees
A naked woman quailing at the knees.

BEAUTY

WITH naught the world contains or small or great
Can we content desire ! " Here is no home !"
Cries Hope—"No realm" cries kingly Love—"No dome !"
Sighs Faith " to tent my altars—alternate
My choruses beneath." They hardly wait,
Though hollow wayside trees hold honeycomb,
Though o'er the hedge-top honeysuckle roam,
But, pilgrims, they push on with " It grows late."
Knowledge they scorn for slowness, and decry
Beauty made happy with a flower's growth,
Beauty whose fault is being sweetly shy,
That, blue-eyed, wonders both at haste and sloth,
That, water-born, was brought up by the light . . .
And yet, O Beauty, touch us with thy might !

AT BETHEL

TO G. E. M.

GABRIEL

Jacob, O Abdiel, the chosen man,
To whom most cheeringly we were revealed,
Ascending and descending ministers
That by a ladder came or went from heaven,—
Jacob has prospered, yet not ceased to err,
Impatient with slow time (his fond belief,
That cunning forwards not retards his ends,
Persisting) and has come, but trembling come,
From Haran back to Bethel: I with him.

Climbed unto fortune by base knavish tricks,
Lured on by darkly guessing ignorance,
Sullen, in torment, he was pleased to meet
Strong opposition from a steady wind:
So made his lonely way on higher ground.
Meanwhile flocks, herds, the camels, asses, dogs,
His hirelings, Leah's train and Rachel's train,
Laid, like the shade of some slow sailing cloud,
Athwart the valley, moved along its bed.

Ah! Abdiel, the light blinds none of us,
Its absence is no barrier to our gaze;
But man's dim eyes are foiled with too much light,
And in the darkness ache, they are so weak:
Not half of what he does doth he intend,
Therefore his purpose must be looked into.
So I was sent to be with him and know
His thought, and I was thrown in doubt—Oh yes!
For, though his ardour conquering obstacles
Has been so great that men astounded tell,
How seven years appeared but a few days
Ere he might win the woman whom he loved;
Yet, compassed by deceits and trivial minds,
Himself did stoop to most unworthy shifts,
And his activity was clouded round
With cares enough, at last, to choke the soul.
Still effort, sprung from anger at himself,
This I perceived to be his saving grace:

Not heaven, not earth, not life doth he distrust,
But doth mistrust himself and for good cause ;
This is his virtue, this his victory.

Leant forward, shoulder edge-wise to the blast,
He made along the rolling sweeps of bleak,
Sad, uncongenial upland, while more fierce
There in his mind a brother's probable wrath
Waxed to predestined certainty and stormed.
He suffered ; and his agony intense
Absorbed me so, that inadvertently,
Foredone with ruth, I almost had been brought
Then to put on the like tormented form
And close with him in answer of his prayer
That strongly yearned to engage some kindred force
And not be lost for ever in the whirl
Which his poor unencountered efforts made.
Although I judged this impulse ill-advised,
Still help, I felt, he needed : help I gave
And met him there with half the host of heaven.
As, when the rain hath ceased some afternoon,
Between a low and deluge-threatening roof
And the wet shining grass that coats the hills,
A space of clarity, a wall of light
Appears as far as eye can reach, each way ;
Thus, with anointed bodies and white spears,
My cohorts in his front emerged to view :
His raised hand shaped a pent-house for his eyes,
Silent he stood and gazed : I signal gave ;
Straight like the boundless shadow when a cloud
Has travelled suddenly across the sun,
Our absence followed where our presence shone.
He said " This is God's host " and named the place.

ABDIEL.
It must be, Gabriel, it must ! This awe,
Beholding energies he might express
Set forth a thousand times with one consent,
Doth show that man begins to know himself.

GABRIEL.

For many days that vision had effect,
While still, as each eve closed, it seemed fair tents
Enriched a sister valley, ere he left
The heights to join his folk who camped below :—
Pavilions, as he deemed them, raised by powers
Watchful for his protection, so he might,
Provided for in the great scheme of things,
Without precaution, buoyantly secure,
Wend on as hand in hand with sun and moon,
Upheld in unison with quiring stars,
His right course found forever, and content.
I bade the wind to cease unneeded then ;
But long it could not be ; the past surged back :
How could he trust those smiling distances ?
It seemed too easy and too magical !
Him gentle airs perplexed yet more than storms,
Who fond would pay a price for pleasant weather :
Acceptance of such generosity
Appeared foolhardy to his teething heart,
Fretful itself supposing fretfulness
In circumambient peace ; the end for him
Loomed darkness, though the end indeed is light.

Wrapped in a head wind's fury he rejoiced
Like one escaped from peril, briefly brave
Ere fears grew gusty : yet an aid welled now,
Within him ; for he thought on Rachel's face.
Perchance thou oft times in the spring hast seen
One tree all white, so tipped it is with buds,
Amongst the tender green of others stand :
O'er him her candour, where most use disguise,
Cast such sweet glamour as that tree exerts ;
And he adored the future in her face.
Gardeners in sultry summer count on fruit,
Rememb'ring how their orchards once were white ;
And recollection of her beauteous youth
Vouched now his ripening fulness, joy and peace.
Alone and undistracted, greatly wrought,
While battling forward on those hills exposed,

He often summoned to his inward view
The beauty that once nerved him to succeed ;
And, to that vision harmonised at once,
His hope spread forth and filled the future up,
Leaving no place for fear : so, from the east,
The magic passage of the light is made
Unto the extremest western verge—no sound,
No stir, attainment without effort—dawn.

ABDIEL

 O Gabriel, man's words take hold on me ;
To hear thee use them touches me to tears.
No stress like this has heavenly intercourse :
Thoughts, passing perfectly from mind to mind
In sacred quiet, mix not pain and pleasure ;
Our songs are silence vivified with awe,
Our weeping is an ecstasy distilled.

GABRIEL

 Even so, dear Abdiel, recall that day,
When first as in a mirror we in Adam
Beheld ourselves expressed in kneaded earth.—
Oh, what a rapt anxiety was ours
To watch his conscious body prove itself !
" Let beauty beautifully move " we sang,
Beholding him stand up in Paradise
Whose many trees were stirred with whispering sound :
The grass was dewy and his feet were pleased ;
His bosom next, conceiving ecstasy,
Filled with the summer wind, and he looked round ;
Vision was his ; but still he raised that hand,
So simple yet so manifold in power, .
Creating by its very aptitude
The thought creative : herewith slow he felt
That breast which to his shoulders slanted up,
To whose firm breadth succeeds the easy neck,
Mobile for stately carriage of his head,
Then seemed to apprehend some heavenly truth
And smiled possessing what so soon proved lost.
 Delighted to hope comprehended thus
In boon and sensuous symbol all we were,

With novel tremor, anxious a first time then,
We sang, and, singing wept, and still we sing,
Weeping, as man's creation still unfolds :
Thus too this man is lyrically stirred
Recalling Rachel young and strange to him.
There, in his mind, I saw her as she came
On foot before her camels, in a stole
Straight, girdleless, of unbleached linen ; large
The opening at the neck in clear ellipse
Lay on her bosom, then swept up, and o'er
Each shoulder vanished ; mellow and warm that lake
Which but just billowed towards each hidden breast ;
Her neck erect seemed strangely slight to rear
The oval head massy with looped up hair
Whose raven depth was crimpled vividly,
In graduated fineness like the track
Cast net-wise out upon some shining pond,
Whose ripple deepens inward from the curve
Its quickened dark forms on that bland expanse—
So from her smooth brow ruffled lobes of hair ;
Guarded by grand shade-treasuring lids and brows
Large pupils, arch for blackness, swam in milk ;
The soft warm cheeks were nowhere flushed or pallid ;
Her lips breath misted ; and, dimpled about with shade,
There, like a rounded pebble, glowed her chin.
Long loose sleeves swaying wholly cloaked her arms ;
While, brown, in green grass-woven sandals cased,
Her feet advancing filled her vesture up
With something like the music of her form,
Audible to the folds it set to move
In grave impressive measures.—Abdiel,
On picturing this, he every time believed,
Despite his stooping to ignoble craft,
That dreamed promise would be all fulfilled,
Redoubling his best efforts to make way ;
For, always strong, the gale would, now and then,
Increase its force so vastly he must halt :
Though difficult steps had yielded him content,
Stopped short or forced to cower near the ground,
The sweat of agony broke from his brow

And drying left strange salt incrusted there.
" O thou, that warring with the furious wind,
Dost symbol forth the passion at thy heart,
That which like cold of serpents frightens thee,
Moist on thy smarting brow, that is thy sweat ;
The dust, thy fingers marvel to find there,
Is salt brought from the glistening desert steppes ;
That sound of scourges is from rags thou wearest,
With which the blast is violent, rousing them
To waspish wrath : O superstitious man,
Build not from these a portent !" So I sighed,
For he prayed abjectly.—"A truce, O wind,
Let him take breath and know himself again."

Yet every eve, having regained the tents,
With brief decisive words he gave command,
Intent to thwart his brother of revenge ;
Dividing first his company in two,
So, were one lost, the other might escape ;
Next sends a noble present on before ;
A second soon of like well-chosen beasts ;
A third anon.—It seemed not right to rest,
And he slept ill ; his life, one over-wrought
Intense conjecture striving to foresee,
Was barred expansion towards his boys and girls ;
E'en Rachel did not venture to draw near.

We came to the ford Jabbok as the dusk
Deepened, what time was left, between these brothers,
Not one day's journey.   Could he rest there, then ?
No, but by moonlight had his droves across ;
The camels bore his wives and children o'er :
Then on the further bank, the camp was pitched.
Yet he crossed not, but palely watched them safe,
Yearning to feel their ease to ford the stream,
A presage and permission for himself :—
And almost prayed he for a sudden squall
To rise, or accident to intervene
With danger from the water, from the winds,
From robber hordes : so did they but succeed
Against some expectation, this might work

Assurance clear, that he would be allowed
To plant his banished feet on native soil ;
Since still instinctive terror held him back
And figured deities of local power,
That in a bounded tract are capable
To harm, and lie in wait for men unsound.
By such might Esau be preferred, he thought,
Whose claim was that of birth, and who besides
Was a swart hunter such as demons love.
These enemies were raised from heathen talk,
When awe which he had watched in alien eyes
Imposed on him despite his better sense.
    Therefore last night, although they safe were crossed,
He climbed unto yon heights, but found no wind
With which to battle and relieve his soul.
I anxiously was near him and I knew,
Almost he would go back : he strained, indeed,
On having crossed his folk and cattle o'er,
As to its moorings in some swollen stream
A shallop doth ; and, as it shakes and sighs,
He moaned and shuddered under stress of fears,
Whose urgent current tugged against his hold—
His failing hold upon the future's strand,
Intent to whirl him backward through the world,
An aimless man to dwindle evermore.

    Then felt I such compulsion to assume
This human form, that very suddenly,
Between his arms outstretched in anguish cruel
To realise his failure setting in—
Yea, that same instant, when I saw with eyes,
His hands were clenched, his elbows bent, his brows
Contracted, and his open mouth and eyes
Drawn with sheer pain to own himself foredoomed !
Feeling this warm resistent wholesome flesh,
Bolt upright, almost touch his out-thrust breast,
He grappled with a cry of bitter joy.
    My thoughts, confused in their strait residence,
Doubted an instant ; whether by this act,
I had not fallen as those others fell,

Who saw the daughters of men how fair they were,
And out of all proportion loved their beauty,
Begetting giants of enormous strength.—
The sympathy I felt had been so strong,
That in the conformation of man's brain,
It found no chamber, save the wards of passion,
Permitting of activity so swift,
Entire, and wholly centred on one end.
Anon that perfect sanity was mine,
Which Enoch reached what time he walked with God,
Grown up to be with us world without end.

    With violence he bound me in his arms,
Then wrestled as it were for very life,
Swinging his weight this side or that of me
To throw or else compel me to my knees :
But I maintained impassively my ground.
And thus it was all night ; his strength grew less,
Yet his will wearied not to conquer now
Or die ; at last, I touched his thigh and caused
The sinew of its hollow to shrink short,
Marking him with full proof, that who opposed,
In rash and strenuous antagonism,
The righted image of his nature's health,
Must lame himself : this blindly yet he did—
Still, still though halt, he persevered in pain,
Though he was weeping, though his arms grew weak
Beyond belief, even as an infant's feeble !
    Yet now at last sobs difficult and heavy
Shook me, no strength of his availed to shake,
And lo ! we staggered tottering both as one ;
For his sobs ruled us in their violence.
Then prayed I him to let me go, since now
The day was breaking.   He with gasps replied
" I will not let thee go, except thou bless me."
" What is thy name ? " I said.   " Jacob," he moaned.
Then I, " Thou shall be called Jacob no more
But Israel ; for like a prince hast thou
Had power with God and men, and hast prevailed."
Silence ensued, but soon he craved yet more :

" Tell me thy name."   " Wherefore is it that thou
After my name shouldst ask ? " was my reproof :
" Content thee that I bless thee ; be thou blessèd."
Herewith I vanished from before his face.

ABDIEL

   O Gabriel, such pains must man endure,
And, hard put to, close always on his fate :
Ay here indeed the generous Esau errs,
Not anxious for the future, nor in throes
Of travail for perfection out of reach.
He met me and mistook me for a youth,
Praised but my beauty, bid me to a meal,
Kissed me and went his way content and kind.

   Thus angels sat, conversing with men's words,
Upon huge stones that strew the higher lawns,
While, in the vale beneath, spread Jacob's tents
And Esau's, side by side in slumber merged.
They were in beauty like to men of strength
One younger, one mature, in perfect health ;
Still we had felt perchance, those limbs had bathed
In sweeter waters than the best on earth.
Most lovely was the night, and they were glad
To take man's beauty to them for a while ;
Yet vanished from their thrones before the dawn
Could rouse one sleeper in those numerous tents.

TWO OF THE LORD'S ANOINTED
TO M. A.

BEFORE the king stood David tall, constrained :
Hot, conscious of presumption, burnt his cheek ;
The king's war-suit an awkward cage he found ;
Young too he felt before the bearded Saul,
And of less moment than beneath the sky
In that rich tent.   The shield of Israel's king
Lay at his feet ; to it the sunlight thrust
Between the tent-skirts, in one vivid wedge,
Making its boss a lamp which gave the place,
Already soaked with sunlight from without,
An airy ampleness—such might be-seem
Some pollen-dusted panoply for bees,
By magic means divorced from the real world,
Down drooping o'er a dream and quite detached
From known events, save that there-under strange,
Ungainly in an armour none of his,
One poised himself mistrustful of its weight ;
Whilst in that bell immense, o'er doubled gold,
His monstrous shadow hover'd vast and pale,
Cast upward by the buckler on the ground.

Though David thus appear to Saul half-dreamed,
His curls are suffering.   Yes, as blossoms, crushed
Beneath a resting ox, yearn for the breeze
To fan, lift and anoint them with cool dew,
Beneath the helm or crisping round its base
His locks recall the oil of Samuel's horn
And pine like flowers estranged from sun and air.
Brown feet alone have freedom and express,
Spurning the carpet's gracious crimson pile,
The great dissatisfaction of his limbs.

Some day he yet may case him suitably
Helping a smith, skilled to embellish arms,
Curve temper'd plates where threads of gold shall run—
Stooping, with naked shoulders gleaming red,
Above the forge : while women stand aloof
And watch the looming shadows of the men
Menaceful lower upon its sooty vault,

And sometimes cry to see fierce sparks spirt up.
Thus underneath the stars they, drawn to watch,
Grouped round a smithy, darkling, treat with Fear :
Saul watches thus, watches a shadow lower
Boastfully overhead, as some loon sways
Gigantic bulk jaunty with drunken mirth ;
And superstitious presage ushers now
Kind fears, now cruel hope through his dark soul.

Much it irked David to be cribbed and caged ;
Like hooded hawk, he brooded in his heart :—
" Nimbly I bounded on the lion's back
And melted naked from the bear's embrace ;
Thus always has my hardihood been free,
Rapid and quick to turn as waters are ;
More swift than freshets find new channels, I
Can thread the boulders or avoid a pit.
But thus, encumbered with his past, I feel
Part-implicated in old worthless deeds.
These straps are stiffened with the sweat of fear ;
In battle dark before the victory
His heart has failed him many times, and now
I feel that these, his fear's accomplices,
No warrant give to stead me hard beset."

A royal tent waits, breathless, for his voice ;
Outside the host chafes for his coming forth ;
Still mute considers him the sullen king ;
While he shrinks in that mail, like blood retreated
With consternation to a leper's heart.

" His gifts, his golden rings weigh now like gyves :
Full oft with delicate meats, with prodigal hand,
He has been good to me, and binds me now.
Sobbed vows, and fruitful tears, and trembling lips
So eager with large promises which since
Have taken root—all these forbid me now.
Oft have I played my harp to quiet him,
And watched his health restored : for what has been
At such times while the palace filled with peace,
Ingratitude will seem aggressive scorn,
And to refuse his help, boy's insolence.

To no man else has my soul come so near :
The evil spirit was gone forth, and Saul
Would draw me close and kiss me while he wept."

That canvas womb warps inward for his voice ;
Yet, tongue-tied, Jesse's son finds nought to urge.

" Pity is powerful, and for a king
So tyrannous, that I despair of grace :
He clings about me like a drowning man,
And both must perish or but one be saved.—
'Tis he is doomed ; there is one only way,
A wrench that needs must cut him like a knife,
Then leave it to his noble energies—
Mutinied unto Fear the renegade,
Who braves more dreadful God and serves with Gath—
To soon or late despatch a helpless king."

Against the splendid housing of a camel
Saul lay absorbed to watch him swayed by doubt ;
Till David said " I cannot go with these,
I have not proved them " ; thereon put them off ;
Then took his staff in silence and went forth,
Letting the curtain fall in such a way
That he and sunlight were shut out at once :
Thus Saul was left alone in gloom and heat.

Some space elapsed ere, sullen blood subdued,
The king of Israel rose as from a dream
And spoke his thoughts : — "O Samson, am I bound ?—
Poor child ! he scorns me—scorns my arms ; poor child !
What beautiful assurance children have !
Such confidence becomes such beauty well !—
Boy, Harper, thou art drunk with ignorance ;
Youth is new wine and makes thee light of head.—
To let him thus go naked to sure death
Proves Cowardice can lay strong hands on Love.
Was I not sure enough he went to death ?—
I whose right place is there, where he now dies ?
The Lord has gone from me, and I grow mean."

He strides about the heavy-coloured gloom
With energetic shudders—to and fro

He strides and shakes his locks, then suddenly
Throws himself on his arms—begins to arm,
Calling to him his slaves, who hark without
And recognise his frenzy's waxing scope,
Through guttural undertone or fuming pause,
To exclamations strangled in their birth ;
Then all, as knowing him too well, withdraw
To watch the tent that like a loaded cloud,
Big with calamity, yet standeth still.

So, in that stifling twilight, none to aid,
But chafed by difficulty, blind with rage,
Saul struggles with his harness, muttering
Like storm full-charged, and thus in some sort arms ;
Till, no more conscious of his neighbourhood,
He draws his sword ; while murd'rous cries that come,
Born far from where the battle breaks at last,
Goad on his fury—soaring to a pitch
Of boundless outrage, acme cruelty—
That arrogance of warriors splashed with blood
Well known to him, pledged deeply to beget
Reliable exultation in his strength.
There, in the stifling twilight of the tent,
Its central mast, hung round with arms and cloaks,
Abnormal, swaggers to his pulsing eyes
And sways convulsive upward from the knees,
As he himself sways, swinging back his sword
To hew Goliath, bodily opposed
To frenzy, which, like prowess undeterred,
Warily circles in, with ringing blows
Struck home and home : until the great mast cracks
And breaking, like a lever slow, descends,
As from palms deadened by repeated shocks
His slanting sword leaves his raised helpless hands ;
While stupefied he feels, with hideous sloth
As of foul vultures settling down at noon,
Full gorged and letting trail their sultry wings,
The great sheets of the tent come folding lower—
Sleepily stoop, then, with huge rush and roar,
Bear down their terror-stiffened prey, close in
Like shelving earth, and so become inert.

IN ELAH

ABNER said " Look, O King ; O Saul, look up.
Rousing his moody majesty, as loth,
The king of Israel saw Goliath's head
Sway slow by David held aloft ; conceived
His youthful pride who, like a maiden, blushed ;
And burned for shame, contrasting with himself,
Fallen from the front, such forward-footing zest.
As though to push the past from out his mind,
Of all its knowledge feigning ignorance,
" Whose son art thou, young man ? " he said and frowned.
But David felt with him and feared his wrath,
So answering knelt " A youngest son am I,
Jesse's, thy servant's, who even now grows old
In Bethlehem."   And Saul rejoined " Go on,
As now thou hast begun ; the Lord of Hosts
Will prosper thee, if thus thou serve me still."
This, Jonathan his son, whose eyes were filled
With David only, judged too poor a meed
And coloured for his father deeply red,
Anon, seized opportunity (despite
The gratulating captains pledging him
Fast as for king's guests flagons can be filled)
To draw nigh-worshipped David from the tent ;
Who (though the giant Gittite's trophied arms,
Holding his gaze, with some demur made slow,
His feet but half consenting to the prince)
Was led beneath the stars till they were come
Some little space without the camp, while calm
The moon rose, shadowing all the vale of Elah,
Yet lavish lapped the slope which, now, they climbed,
Making its dew all diamonds, in light
Gentle as was the heart of Jonathan.
He hung his arms round David, dumb with love,
And wept tears brighter than the radiant dew
Which, dripped, shone on the unadornèd neck
Of that victorious youth ; to whom he said
In woman-like distress " Be thou my friend :
Ah ! pledge thy soul to mine, whose pledge foregone,

Whether disdained or treasured, must be thine."
Stopped so and, holding David at arm's length,
Laughed ; for the moon frustrated his fond gaze,
Refulgent from behind a curled eclipse :
Then forced him turn until enchantress rays
Caressed a beauty matchless thus (for wonder
Breathing a little quick, a little flushed
With pride) and gazing could not speak at all :—
Eyes, black as the hooding hair and wide apart,
Reposed as on lands promised ; lip with lip,
As when pomegranate bursts, had kissed and smiled
Parting ; nostrils and brows decisive soared,
Like eagle wings active anew each dawn,
Through confidence, as through a settled weather :
All which cast glamour upon captive eyes.
But David, whose shrewd sense had oft appraised
That charm of bearing owned by the king's son—
Had envied even manners more refined,
Gained in a station constantly observed—
Touched too by those fond words—elate to feel
So good a mainstay for his gadding hopes
Come to his hand with proffered service free—
Bent quickly forward, kissed a shadowed face
And found it wet with tears of love for him.
So they embraced and joining hands did vow
To be bond brothers, both in life and death
True to each other's good.   " As the Lord liveth,
So long as thy soul liveth and my soul,
In every peril, by the ark and by
Jehovah whose it is, I vow" each said.
In nervous hurry Jonathan unclasped
His burnished girdle, stammering "'Tis thine",
Already tugging at his baldrick's buckles ;
Which loosed, his sword fell noisy to the ground
While he unbrooched his cloak.   " Take, give me thine ; "
He gasped " For these shall witness to our oath."
Then David slipped his single shepherd-smock
And stood all naked by the soft moon bathed
In milky radiance, swart Astarte's veil,
Whom Tyrians deem love's froward queen in heaven ;

While Jonathan stopped short to gaze on him.
Holding a belt of brass in either hand
(One Abner's gift, one which himself now gave)
There David stood, five bracelets on each arm—
Goodwill of warrior hearts won utterly
That day.   He stood, in country sandals shod,
A supple youth with clear, fawn-coloured skin :
His dimpled joints were braced, not knotted yet ;
Soft as rich bruises in an opal stone,
His veins, where'er least bedded, blue bespoke
Full buoyancy of health ; his thighs curved firm
Like ivory tusks, which polished smooth, support
The throne of Pharaoh's queen ; his feet pressed down,
As on warm wax a monarch's thumb sets seal
To leave quite plain a walled town's warrant there :
From his head's crown to his foot's palm, no fault
Flawed gradual harmony—no woman ever
More of a piece in beauty could be dreamed.
So Jonathan took breath to gaze at him ;
Then loosed his silken tunic, one by one
Put off his chains and laid his ear-rings by,
To stand by David's side, more equal now
In all but beauty.   Being something older,
Less even was the progress of his form :
Its structure, wrested from a kindlier bent—
Too rigidly compact through early drill
Self-forced to please his father and grown men—
Broke, almost violent, on knee or hip
Mature ; his wiry arms swung hands too large.
The shoulders much redeemed all such defects,
For they were royal as his bearing was ;
And features, set in perseverance strict,
By patience tempered, here and there acute,
Claimed kindred with staid aspects of far peaks.
Exiled from peace by constant exigence
His spirit peered through dark distended doors,
Though little nursed of leisure, still unweaned
By action's prompting from its primal food.
Scant curls he had and lips not full ; yet all
But hampered in his face undaunted zest

That kept him, younger than his years, a child.
So side by side they stood beneath the stars,
While camp fires thick in shadowed Elah glowed
And, now and then, afar some jackal yelped,
Or lion howled come down to tear the slain
Left fallen o'er the rough land's ups and downs
Even to Shaaraim, Gath and Ekron.
They stood, while time ran on till all the hills
Were as a presence with composure grand—
Till the whole witnessing heavens stood away
More vast, while the horizon slipped all bounds.
Then suddenly the air was cold to them,
And they lost comfort dwindling from touched peace.
Silently each put on the other's dress :
Jonathan, ready first, helped smiling David
Puncture each ear and through the delicate lobe
Thrust safe the bending gold of ear-rings rich,
Whereon some tiny dots of spirted blood,
Appearing added rubies, paled his cheek
More than swamped gore of ruthless victories ;
Then gravely hand in hand he led him back.

Of their encounters in the past day's course
Both, full, were chatting ere the camp was reached ;
When after half an hour, by fireside spent,
Where Michal sat and listened near her brother,
They sought their beds to sleep off the fatigue.

Thus closed for Jonathan his brightest day ;
But David's fortunes barely peeped as yet.

JONATHAN
TOGETHER with and stretched before the sun
A large white veil of cloud moved up the east,
For placid shining like a wall of snow.
The sky, in travail to bring forth the light,
Long since had paled : all stones and rocks were moist,
Shoulder and cliff austere loomed shadowless,
Grass rustled bleak, the wind swept on and on.
Still Jonathan kept silent, and his page
But shuddered, rubbed his watery eyes or gaped.
From westward close abreast three eagles toiled,
In the wind's teeth advancing slow (long since,
As drowned in milk, all stars had dimmed from sight) ;
Alone their wing'd strength to the zenith came ;
Them the sun gilded there ; they shone in heaven,
Though still that cloud-veil sundered every hill
From glow and warmth. 'Twas thus that day began
While Jonathan went forth into the field.
An omen from those royal birds he drew ;
For two forsook their course, though one held on
Golden, exulting to approach the sun.
So David would, but he and Saul must first
Turn back—a weary bitter thought for him.

He took his bow and arrows from the boy
And aimed as at a mark and hit the stone,
Ezel, or missed, for some half dozen shots :
Then said " Go fetch them in."   Off ran the lad
And gathered the five nearest ; for the sixth
Gazed all about : when Jonathan cried loud
" The arrow is beyond thee !   Haste thee, haste ! "
The boy came back : to whom his archer-kit
Saul's son resigned, and bade him take them home.
Now nothing guessed the lad, and went, well pleased
Soon to consort with company less grave ;
But David knew.
                    Rooted, yet ill at ease,
Alone there Jonathan remained, and stood
As in Sidonian palace there might stand,
What time the bitter factions fly to arms,

A Princess, for whose hand their leaders strive :—
Birth, blood, associations, these pronounce
For some gloomed merchant-king whose heart has soured,
Whose mind has warped through years of pride at bay ;
Her love and youth plead for some gallant prince,
As Jonathan's for David, eloquent ;
And—as with love's true choice fain would converse
That heart disputed, saving that she knows
All walls have ears, while every cranny's dark
Seems deep with the set hatred of an eye,—
So Jonathan is fain of David's words.
Life's kindling charm both feel ; To-morrow's spell
Is on them ; Hope sets tingling both their ears
With shame to think, how those who claim their duty
Live darkly—hate and dread the future :—Ay,
As she might yield, though fearing crueller gods,
Accused at heart for hopes endangering love,
In dread to hear gay spurs clink where Death lurks,
Or miss the signal of so boon approach ;
Even so did Jonathan remain, accused
By love for hope, endowing with vile eyes
The breathing voiceless waste, in dread to hear
Or fail of hearing, quick-advancing steps
Whose sound he loved.   Slave of prolonged desire,
He ached for David dangerously hid.—
Should friend risk friend ?   Why did he wait and tempt
With plausible bliss to probable bane his friend ?
Why should he send the lad away alone ;
And treacherously there with face of safety
Seem to expect contempt of life from Love ?
What Hatred might desire, yearned he for that ?

Long, long he stood thus gazing on the ground,
At issue between love and need of love,
Though now the sun had rent that cloud to shreds
And shines full in his face—though David risen
From mid rocks to the south which hold the shade,
There waits till he shake off that downcast mood.

Late then, with wretched heart, he peered all round.

But dazzled could not pierce within the shade ;
Which seeing, David stepped forth toward the sun
And stood before the shadowy clefts lit up :
When Jonathan cried loud as heathen maids,
To hail that star they worship, shuddering cry,
Because they deem it virile and a god
Prompt to take umbrage at their virgin state.
But David touched his brow to earth three times,
Prostrate before his prince—drew near, and they
Embraced, kissing each other while they wept.
It was with them no time for many words :
Sobbed Jonathan " He cast his spear at me—
Said thou wouldst take my kingdom ; and in truth
Thou wouldst and wilt. . . . Hast thou had food enough
And all things needful in the wilderness ?"
And David, "Yea ; save love : thou lov'st me still ?
Swear that. Outcast am I and meet no smile,—
Need words to ponder." Jonathan cried : " Words !
Are brothers starved on words ? Alas, alas !"
And so they wept one on the other's neck
Till David, he exceeded ; for his lot
Seemed quite dependent on the prince's love :
Grief's cause, not hourly thrust upon him, surged
The less familiar, causing heavier bursts ;
Therefore he well might weep beyond his friend.
But Jonathan, not jealous of his woe,
His own so mastered him, soothingly said
" Now go in peace, for both of us have sworn,
Ay, both before Jehovah spake aloud
' The Lord between thee be and me, between
My seed and thine for ever !' Haste thee ! haste
There will be shepherds here, his spies anon,
Who must not learn that thou art yet hard by :
Thy murderer my father shall not be !
Choose lonely paths, be speedy !" David then
Arose and sought the wilderness alone ;
But Jonathan stood still, as though he deemed
To feel his sorrow lift, when David should
At last be out of sight. So by her child,
Though told that it is dead, a mother stands :

Until the little body move again,
She means to wait.   Thus Jonathan felt bound
Though David was no longer e'en in sight.

There were the sullen rocks and basking tracks
Which torrents trample twice a year ; there were
The tiny tongueless flowers ; mute earth was there :
But skies were distant radiant and serene.
His hungry eyes communed with solitude :
Yet found that arching confidence no friend,
But something cruel ; and the urgent wind
Insistent out of season chafed his soul.

Turning at last, he hated as he turned,
Or knew he loathed first, setting face that way,
His father's house ; where Malady enthroned
Misruled ; then Passion, magic in resource,
Set round him darksome halls sumptuous in vain :
Thick curtains heaved, and slaves from hiding cringed ;
Impotent obstacles, dumb for revenge,
Rucked carpets, upset seats, witnessed tongue-tied ;
All, supplicating health for obvious guilt,
His own wife, concubines and wives of Saul,
Together huddled, kissed the Teraphim,
And prayed aghast ; like conies 'mong the rocks,
Sad children, peeped from holes and corners, scared ;
The evil spirit held its own within,
Where, God-abandoned, suffered, brute-like, Saul.
He hated all who dwelt abjectly there—
He could not go ; the bitter hills were best !

But wizard passion juggled with stern rocks
And built conjectural dens, where David slept
While leisurely a lion snuffed him round.—
Lo ! waking he cries out—grips the rough mane
With nightmare desperation—struggles hard,
At disadvantage, cramped !—When David's blood
Mottled that tawny pelt, against his eyes
Jonathan dashed both hands, beside himself
At traitor visions, dark'ning them with pain.
Instant reprisal ! galled, their balls made surge
The frenzied Saul, javelin poised aloft

To cast at David knelt beside his harp . . .
How David strained to rise, avoid sheer death !
And could not—could not move ! Yet the dart flew—
But faster Jonathan upon his eyes
Vehemently smote both hands in sequent blows,
Till wandering tears came salt into his mouth,
While his breast heaved with yearning to evolve
New shapes more apt for tumult in distress,
Capacious for the woes of womanhood !

Up in the hills and far from any help,
Now sank he down prone as a thwarted child.—
Next watched he David come where aliens dwelt,
Scorned as a thing of nought—by servants gibed—
Upon the threshold stone bid to a seat—
No better fed than dogs ; for tattered he
Limped jaded from forced walking—dimmed with dust,
His beauty drew not even women's eyes,
But passed unguessed at with his strength foreworn.
Jonathan longed to sack that cold walled town ;
Sorely he pitied David, but hard fate,
Clogged like congealed blood round a throbbing wound,
Pinched tenderness. Sometimes a bear, though chained,
Refuses to grow callous of restraint,
But wears its feet in dogged back and forth—
Nor spurred, nor checked by pain, still bleeding churns
Each raw palm in a socket of red sand,
As drugged by suffering, torpid with stale ache
Heaving its mill-stone weight from side to side :
Thus his huge leaden grief ground his maimed thoughts
In their worn prints on hateful circumstance.

Why was he not with David sharing all ?
Why stood his father wholly in his way?
Ah, was his mother shamed in him, who proved
Enemy of their house—foe to himself?
Was hers illicit offspring—tainted blood
Of undiscovered sin, discovered now
By his rebellious, by his impious hand ?
Will love break bridle? Was his late career
Her passionate failure's echo? Thought refused

The summons which such accusations dinned ;
Though Saul in maddened rage last night declared
Him " Son of her rebellion—Her confusion—.
Her nakedness uncloaked," had called him that,
And cast suspicion as a net is cast.
In clinging degradation knotted now,
He labours lion-like to wound himself;
And reads love's meaning less in life preserved
Than wanton danger and self-violence :
Deems death the hidden sense of warmest vows,
The gibbet-goal of every tedious life.

    Why was he not with David sharing all ?
Ah ! David dared not ask ; and for that cause
Exceeded him in tears.—

                 His spear was up !
Had singled out a sheep strayed browsing nigh :
So hated he all lives that showed content !
But sudden panic at his purposed deed
Caught back the shaft ; wholly his father's son,
Had now the evil spirit entered him?
By conscience-stricken terror numbed lest he,
Ay, even he, found capable anon
Of treason, masking suicide, might choose
Some hot mêlée to run on David's sword -
And curse him so ; or, mad with pain prolonged
As Saul, who loved, now hated, monstrously
Contrive cold perjuries to blast his friend.—
Humbling his face in dust he quaked to think
His child was lame—born with unusual throes,
As though the womb reluctantly brought forth
Life doomed to failure.   Ah ! was he a curse
Unto his son, his father, and his friend ?—
Wronged his heart closed-to like a heavy tomb,
While both eyes stiffened as in mortar set.

    How beautiful was David !   How beloved !
Himself as one forgotten must stand by
Where David was—take rank as David's friend.
To honour Israel's bounty from the Lord
The mothers bade their rosy broods clap hands—

Give "Saul his thousands, David his ten thousands"—
And sing him past their doors ; fair maidens stood
Thoughtful upon a sudden or grew brisk
Flushed with some new anxiety to charm ;
Men gave him gifts on gifts, not finding words
That could express meet worship for such bright
Full revelation of success in life.—
"Yet am I king's son. . . . Ah ! but Saul is king !"
Hereon his love he bitterly recalled
Since their first vows, and all his sister's love ;
How both had stood between their father's wrath
And David, yet was he no wit more safe !
" Beloved but for my sheer love's sake am I
Who love, for David's own sake, David so."
He groaned, yet owned himself unworthy love :
He wept, but then the kindness of the Lord
Came home to him and raised him to his feet—
" What need I, being blessed, as I am blessed,
To live in these same years that make thy life ?
Not born before to loveless ignorance,
Nor to regret too late ?—O God most high,
I worship Thee for timing thus my days :
White-haired I might have seen his grace and died
Reluctant, unregretted—or a child
Have watched his feeble age belie his fame
Degrading him to my companionship !"

He spoke aloud and breathed the air as one
Who goes forth to the wedding of his friend.—
In ancient days of vague renown what name
Might match with his who slew the giant ?—what
Rival his friend's, deserving costlier work
Of ivory inlaid and framed with gold
To hang up near the ark, which Levites, pale
With awful knowledge, learnedly might spell
To generations yet unborn and show
The casque and brazen greaves, the weavers' beam—
Five thousand shekels' weight of cumbrous mail—
Huge sword that clave its wielder's neck in twain—
Last, David's sling and scrip with still four pebbles.—

Ah, was he not yet nimble to go on,
Naught out of reach, no dream too absolute?
Where David brings his beauty into view,
Who erst ignored that head anointed, learns
It must have been, approving God's design.
Ah! what might not be done and he, Saul's son
Witness the glory of it! Nay, himself,
Second to none but David, share the praise!
  Straightway he vowed, that henceforth this thought ever
Should, summoned at his need, succour his soul
When compassed round by baleful circumstance:
Then, for a space lost, wondered at the calm
Of those lone slopes browsed o'er by sheep and goats,
(For since the sun with full-noon mightiness
Had cowed the hills, needs must a lax bland smile
Simmer o'er all) yet, resolute, soon turned
From where the shepherd lets his days glide by—
No David in event to make dreams real,
But past his prime e'en then; and with high thoughts
Footed it downward toward the deep-drowsed vale.

A TRANSLATION

DOVES, from the palm-trees near them, gently cooed,
While other birds made short flights through the grass :
Ringed galeoles, and quails from Tarshish brought,
And Punic guinea-fowl.   Untended long,
The garden was with bushy verdure clogged ;
For bitter-apples, gourds and cucumbers
Had climbed among the boughs of cassia-trees,
Milk-weed and swallow-wort were dotted through
The rose beds, every kind of trailing growth
Looped down in leafy cradles interlaced ;
And slant rays, as in woods, threw here and there
The shadow of a leaf distinctly shaped
Upon the ground.   Tamed beasts, grown wild once more,
Fled off at the least sound.   Sometimes one watched
A shy gazelle with little black hooves drag
The peacock feathers, scattered all about,
Some distance down the paths.   And, far away,
The clamour of the town droned, all but merged
With the waves' roar.   The sky was wholly blue ;
And not a sail in sight upon the sea.

HERE ENDS THE VINEDRESSER AND OTHER POEMS. PRINTED BY MORRISON & GIBB, LIMITED, EDIN-BURGH, FOR THE UNICORN PRESS, VII CECIL COURT, ST. MARTIN'S LANE, LONDON, W.C.

*9 7 8 3 7 4 4 7 2 2 6 8 1 *